Dimity Duck

To Aaron, Brett, and Lexi, Hunter, Hayden, and Maya,
my newest grandnieces and nephews— J.Y.

Pour Lise—S.B.

PHILOMEL BOOKS
A division of Penguin Young Readers Group.
Published by The Penguin Group.
Penguin Group (USA) Inc., 375 Hudson Street, New York, NY 10014, U.S.A.
Penguin Group (Canada), 90 Eglinton Avenue East, Suite 700, Toronto, Ontario, Canada M4P 2Y3
(a division of Pearson Penguin Canada Inc.).
Penguin Books Ltd, 80 Strand, London WC2R 0RL, England.
Penguin Ireland, 25 St. Stephen's Green, Dublin 2, Ireland (a division of Penguin Books Ltd.).
Penguin Group (Australia), 250 Camberwell Road, Camberwell, Victoria 3124, Australia (a division of Pearson Australia Group Pty Ltd).
Penguin Books India Pvt Ltd, 11 Community Centre, Panchsheel Park, New Delhi - 110 017, India.
Penguin Group (NZ), Cnr Airborne and Rosedale Roads, Albany, Auckland 1310, New Zealand (a division of Pearson New Zealand Ltd).
Penguin Books (South Africa) (Pty) Ltd, 24 Sturdee Avenue, Rosebank, Johannesburg 2196, South Africa.
Penguin Books Ltd, Registered Offices: 80 Strand, London WC2R 0RL, England.

Library of Congress Cataloging-in-Publication Data
Yolen, Jane. Dimity Duck / Jane Yolen ;
illustrated by Sebastien Braun.—1st American ed.   p. cm.
Summary: Dimity Duck and Frumity Frog have a fun day together in the pond,
then go home when it gets dark outside.
[1. Ducks–Fiction. 2. Frogs–Fiction. 3. Play–Fiction. 4. Friendship–Fiction. 5. Stories in rhyme.]
I. Braun, Sebastien, ill. II. Title.   PZ8.3.Y76Di 2006   [E]–dc22   2005034619

ISBN 0-399-24632-0
1 3 5 7 9 10 8 6 4 2

Dimity Duck

by Jane Yolen

illustrated by Sebastien Braun

Philomel Books

Dimity Duck
waddles,
she **toddles**
out of bed.

Niddy-noddy
goes her tail
and *quack!*
goes her
head.

She **brushes** all
her feathers,
as gold as
new-mown
hay,

then smiles into
her mirror.

It's time to start
the day.

Dimity Duck
waddles,
she **toddles**
off to eat.

Wiggle-
waggle
goes her
tail
and pump! go her feet.

She paddles off to breakfast. She dines on fish and weeds.

She finds
that
in the deep
blue pond
is all
the food
she
needs.

Dimity Duck waddles,
she toddles
and she sings.

Giggle-gaggle
goes her
tail

and whoosh!

go her
wings.

Frumity Frog watches,

he splashes

in the pond.

He **waves** a foot at Dimity,
of whom he's
very fond.

Dimity Duck waddles,
she paddles to his side.

Splishy-splashy
go the two,
playing
seek-and-hide.

All day they play till Frog decides
to hide beneath a pad.

Dimity Duck
    can't find him,
and *sniff!*
    she's feeling
            sad.

Surprise!

Dimity Duck
waddles,

 she dawdles

and she dips.

She **showers** her
friend Frumity
with **frithy-frothy**
drips.

Frumity Frog
giggles,
he
wriggles
with
delight.

He
bubbles
and he
babbles
but–it's

getting on

toward

night.

Dimity Duck waddles,
she toddles
and grows
pale.

Drifty-drafty goes
her head
and **droop!**
goes her tail.

She throws
her friend
big kisses
as the sun sinks
out of sight.

For Dimity
and
Frumity,
playtime
ends
with night.

Dimity Duck
wadd les,
she gets
into her
gown.

She makes
her bed
and
plumps her
pillows
full of
eiderdown.

Dimity Duck
waddles,

she **toddles**
off to bed.

Sleepy-sloppy goes her tail . . .

. . . and snore goes her head.

Good night, Dimity.

Shhhhhhhhhhh!